KIDS CAN'T STOP READING THE CHOOSE YOUR OWN ADVENTURE STORIES!

"Choose Your Own Adventure is the best thing that has come along since books themselves."
—Alysha Beyer, age 11

"I didn't read much before, but now I read my Choose Your Own Adventure books almost every night."
—Chris Brogan, age 13

"I love the control I have over what happens next."
—Kosta Efstathiou, age 17

"Choose Your Own Adventure books are so much fun to read and collect—I want them all!"
—Brendan Davin, age 11

And teachers like this series, too:

"We have read and reread, worn thin, loved, loaned, bought for others, and donated to school libraries our Choose Your Own Adventure books."

CHOOSE YOUR OWN ADVENTURE®— AND MAKE READING MORE FUN!

CHOOSE YOUR OWN ADVENTURE® • 158

ILLUSTRATED BY TOM LA PADULA

BANTAM BOOKS
NEW YORK • TORONTO • LONDON • SYDNEY • AUCKLAND

RL4, age 10 and up

SKY-JAM!

A Bantam Book / April 1995

CHOOSE YOUR OWN ADVENTURE® is a registered trademark of Bantam Books, a division of Bantam Doubleday Dell Publishing Group, Inc. Registered in U.S. Patent and Trademark Office and elsewhere.

Original conception of Edward Packard
Cover art by Jeff Mangiat
Interior illustrations by Tom La Padula

ISBN 0-553-56623-7

Published simultaneously in the United States and Canada

Bantam Books are published by Bantam Books, a division of Bantam Doubleday Dell Publishing Group, Inc. Its trademark, consisting of the words "Bantam Books" and the portrayal of a rooster, is Registered in U.S. Patent and Trademark Office and in other countries. Marca Registrada. Bantam Books, 1540 Broadway, New York, New York 10036.

PRINTED IN THE UNITED STATES OF AMERICA

OPM 0 9 8 7 6 5 4 3 2 1

SKY-JAM!

WARNING!!!

Do not read this book straight through from beginning to end. These pages contain many different adventures you may have on and off the court as an up-and-coming player on one of the hottest high-school basketball squads in the country.

From time to time as you read along, you'll have the chance to make a choice. You are responsible for the adventures you have because you choose. After you make a decision, follow the directions to find out what happens to you next.

Think carefully before you act. You could lead your team to a winning season, win attention from college scouts, even play for the state championship! But it will take discipline, determination, and some heads-up ball-handling to be a star. You will be called upon to make split-second decisions that could mean the difference between triumph and defeat. Do you have what it takes?

Good Luck!

"Well, there it is," your dad says. You gaze up at the hoop and freshly painted backboard mounted over the garage door. The rim is exactly ten feet above the ground. It looks higher.

"Thanks for putting it up," you say, but he's already passing the ball. You catch it and dribble in, then jump as high as you can. The ball slides off your fingers, hits the backboard, and bounces off the rim. You take the rebound, elevate, and hit a high, arching jump shot from the baseline. The snap of the net echoes in your ears as you bring your arms down slowly in front of you. You are in the groove.

The hum of crickets in your backyard fades into the hum of cheering fans in your high-school gym. Focusing on your memory of that perfect shot, once again you reach for a high, arching baseline jumper. Only this time it rattles out.

As you hustle back on defense, you wonder if maybe you shouldn't have been thinking about shooting hoops all alone in your driveway. This is the next-to-last game of the season for Windham, your school team, and hard as you practice, things just aren't coming together for you yet.

A Davenport player grabs the rebound, fires it downcourt to their forward. A second later his points instead of yours go up on the scoreboard.

Turn to page 2.

You hustle to keep up. You get off a few good passes and drive in uncontested for an easy layup. A few minutes later you try for a three-pointer. It whirls around the rim before spinning out. The action is fast and wild. You give it all your worth, but you can't find your groove. The final buzzer sounds with Windham barely squeaking through what should have been an easy win.

Coach Garafalo passes you coming out of the locker room. He's a big guy with tousled hair, full of energy. During the games he's always pacing up and down, punching the palm of one hand with the fist of the other.

"Sorry I wasn't on today, Coach," you say.

He doesn't answer, just glowers under his bushy gray eyebrows. But later, in the locker room, he takes you aside. "Look," he says. "This is how it stands. If you expect any court time in the big one against Carthage next week, you'll have to show me a lot more in the scrimmage on Saturday."

You're feeling pretty low as you wait for the bus after school, wondering if you're suffering from burnout, washed up after just your first year on the squad.

The bus arrives. You're about to get on when Fred Stauffer, a friend of yours, comes up.

"You'll never guess what I just found out," he says.

"What?"

Go on to the next page.

"Guess who's coming to Windham? Only Jeffrey Gordon."

"Jeffrey Gordon—*the* Jeffrey Gordon—you're putting me on."

"No, honest. His mother just moved here, and Jeffrey is coming to help her get settled. Don't tell anyone—we don't want any big crowds following us—but Bob Rosewald found out where the house is! Bob and I are planning to hang out there Saturday to see if we can get him to give us his autograph. Maybe he'll even give us a few basketball tips. I hear he loves kids. Want in?"

"You mean it?" You ponder what Fred has just told you. It means that the town of Windham is going to be famous—well, sort of famous. Jeffrey Gordon retired a couple of years ago, but he's considered to be one of the greatest basketball players of all time, maybe *the* greatest. Everywhere he goes is news. And the fact that his mother will be living in your town, and Jeffrey will be coming to visit sometimes—well, that's something!

"What do you say?" Fred asks.

You wince as you remember the practice game. "Saturday is the team's last big drill before the Carthage game," you say.

Turn to page 97.

Windham has worked especially hard on inbound plays. And by the middle of the third quarter it pays off. Your team catches Lakeside unawares on a few key inbounds passes downcourt, converts on a few turnovers, and moves out to an eight-point lead.

The streak is broken when a Windham forward is called for traveling, and Lakeside answers with two points. Then when Windham takes the ball down on your next possession, a Lakeside player reaches around and bats the ball clean out of your teammate's dribbling hand, takes it, and drives hard toward the basket. You're in his way and in position, but he spins, twists, steps back over the three-point line and lofts it for a tré. Your lead is cut to three.

Windham's possession again. The ball comes to you this time. You bring it back up the court. You notice that your center is moving into place to set a pick on your defender. With a quick crossover dribble you could use the pick and drive straight up the lane for a layup, but out of the corner of your eye you notice another teammate wide open from three-point range. An easy pass outside could be a safer bet, and a successful three-pointer would shift the momentum of the game back to you. What to do? You need to score here to protect your lead.

If you decide to use the pick,
turn to page 25.

If you decide to pass,
turn to page 38.

You don't mention your phone call to Coach Bartok, but a few days later he stops you in the hall. "Got a minute before your next class?"

"Sure Coach, what's up?"

"I got a call last night from Coach Garafalo at Windham—he said you'd phoned and asked if there could be an exhibition game between our two schools. He said he could arrange everything if the Spring Rock principal and I approved."

"Great!" you exclaim. "Is it okay then?"

"I'm afraid not," Bartok says. "First of all—you had no business making such a call. That's my job, I'm the coach. It looks odd to have a student making a call like that."

"I'm sorry," you say. "I guess I should have talked to you more, but you did say it would be nice if we could have a game with Windham. I thought it would be all right."

"It *would* be nice," Bartok says. "But that doesn't mean it's possible. The fact is, Windham is a much bigger, faster team than we are. They're *two* leagues ahead of us. We'd get whipped—there's a real danger of injuries in a game like that. It would be bad morale for our players at a crucial time in the season. And the game would be boring for all the people who came to watch it."

You feel so depressed listening to all this that you don't know what to say.

Turn to page 83.

"Sometimes I wish I were too, Coach," you say.

"What you suggest—this exhibition game—would be very unusual."

"Yes, well, I was afraid it wouldn't work out," you say.

"I didn't say it wouldn't work out," the coach snaps back. "I said it would be very unusual. But there's nothing wrong with doing something unusual. We could announce it as a special charity game—say, to help raise funds for the new hospital."

"That would be great," you say. "I have to admit I mentioned the idea to our coach, and he didn't think it would be possible."

"I'm sure he'll be all for it," Garafalo says. "I'll discuss it with our principal here at Windham, and if he gives the go-ahead, I'll check it out with your coach myself."

"That's great—thanks," you say.

"And thanks for calling," he says. "I'll be in touch."

Turn to page 15.

SPRING ROCK
PHYS. ED.
WINDHAM PHYSICAL ED. DEPT

Your body answers with a rush of adrenaline as you decide to go for the dunk. You palm the ball in one hand, drive in the way you've practiced, and leap—too soon! You know it as soon as you've left the ground. Your reach falls short, and your hand slams against the rim, sending the ball straight up in the air as you tumble out-of-bounds. You look up in time to see your teammate come down with the offensive rebound and lay the ball up against the backboard for a sure two points.

Turn to page 17.

Jeffrey squats down a bit so you don't have to crane your neck to talk to him. "Hey," he says, "if you were able to grab the limb of that tree, you're going to be able to grab the rim of a basket someday."

Jeffrey's friend, who looks familiar but whom you can't quite recognize, comes over. "Just takes motivation," he says.

They had plenty of that just now," Jeffrey says, grinning.

Bob and Fred come over and cluster next to you.

"Climbed over the fence?" Jeffrey asks.

You nod.

"I thought so. Well, don't tell any more of your friends to try it. They might have to spend all night in a tree."

Bob and Fred laugh nervously.

"Look," Jeffrey says. "I can't talk now—I promised to help my mother with some things. Don't climb over any more fences—you can go out the drive." He grins. "The guard might bite you even though the dogs won't, but I'll tell him you're friends of mine."

"Thanks, Jeffrey," you say, still slightly in awe.

"No problem. You kids play school ball?"

Turn to page 74.

"Yeah, but they're *my* two seasons," you say. "Why can't we set up a game against Windham? They're right in the same town, after all."

"That would be nice, but it's just not in the cards. Windham is not only in the A league, they're one of the best in that league. They're contenders for the state championship—"

"All the more reason to play them," you interrupt.

Coach Bartok drapes a hand over your shoulder. "Look. I know you're anxious to test yourself, but sometimes in life you've got to be content with what you have. You're having a great season. Relax and enjoy it."

You break away from him and head for the locker room. He was only trying to be kind, but he didn't make you feel the slightest bit better. You've half a mind to call Coach Garafalo at Windham yourself and ask if he'd be willing to schedule an exhibition game. Would that ever be great! Just to see how well Spring Rock could do!

Turn to page 88.

SPRING
ROCK
PHYS.
ED.
SPRING
ROCK
PHYS.
ED.
SR

COUNTY
SCIENCE
FAIR
E=MC2

You never thought you could get so interested in something like this, but working on your science fair project gives you as good a feeling as winning a basketball game.

A couple of weeks later you get an even better feeling: winning a big glass trophy with "$E=mc^2$" engraved on it for the outstanding high-school entry in your county's science fair. And later that spring you win a science scholarship to the state university!

On graduation day, Coach Bartok comes up to you after the commencement ceremony. He looks down at his shoes for a moment, then says, "I've been wanting to tell you—I think I made a mistake cutting you off about lining up a game with Windham. I still feel bad about your having quit the team."

"That's okay, Coach," you say. "Things are working out pretty well for me."

"I'm glad of that," he says. "Tell me, are you going to go out for basketball in college?"

"I might," you say.

"Think about it," he says. "You could have what it takes to jam with the best."

The End

"Let's just wait here," you say. "I don't think the guard will call the police. If he does, the worst that can happen is that they'll tell us to move off."

"The worst that can happen is we'll get bored waiting and Jeffrey Gordon, basketball legend, will slip right by us behind tinted windows," Fred says.

"Relax. We'll move in closer gradually," Bob says. "He's got to stop while the guard opens the gate, doesn't he?"

At that moment the guard, who had gone back into his little house, comes out again. He glances over at you, then holds up a cellular phone and starts talking.

"You think he's calling the cops?" Fred says.

"Maybe he's just bluffing—trying to scare us off," you say.

"He's got to do something to feel important," Bob says.

Ten minutes or so pass, and no cops come. The guard is in his guardhouse. Bob nods at you and Fred and nudges his bike a few feet closer to the end of the drive. You are about to do the same when over your shoulder you notice a sleek sedan with a bright silvery finish slowing as it approaches the entrance. The windows are half open. There are two men in it—big men. The driver is Jeffrey Gordon!

Turn to page 48.

As you hang up, you feel a rush of excitement and anticipation, but there's still something nagging you: should you tell Coach Bartok about having called Coach Garafalo yourself? You certainly don't feel like telling him—he'll probably be annoyed. On the other hand, maybe you should come clean.

If you tell Coach Bartok about the phone call you made, turn to page 29.

If you decide against it, turn to page 5.

SPRING
ROCK
44
WINDHAM
11
SPRING
ROCK
24

The ball is quickly back in action despite your hurt pride. For a moment it's a seesaw game, with turnovers on each side, then Spring Rock has it again. A teammate passes to you, and you drive down.

A defender moves in. You step into him, then step back and fake right, then drive past him. Another defender moves in to guard you. You wheel and circle back. He's still on you. You bounce pass to a forward and race in. The forward rifles it back to you, and you move in hard and force the layup for two points. It feels good to come back strong after missing before.

Next time defending, Windham shoots, misses, and the forward tries to tip it in. It rolls off the rim. Your center snares the ball with a flying leap, gives it to a forward, and you're all moving downcourt.

You cut across the lane and take a pass from a forward at the far post. You dish it off to the shooting guard. He's stopped. The ball comes back to you. You lose your defender with a crossover dribble, then cock your arm and push the ball up and away for a three-pointer. *Swoosh.* What a feeling! The Windham fans are quieting down and Spring Rock is back in the game.

Turn to page 96.

You decide against calling Coach Garafalo. Although you're dying to test your skills, going behind Coach Bartok's back just isn't the way to do it. Instead, you focus on your remaining league games and concentrate on becoming the best basketball player in Spring Rock history.

Alumni Day comes. This is when former students come back to visit the school and watch the game between Spring Rock and its old rival, Cooperstown. The game is a walkover. Spring Rock wins by twenty-three points. Not bad, you think. Except Cooperstown didn't have much of a team.

A recent graduate—Mike Faber—comes up to you after the game. "I didn't know Spring Rock had such a great team," he says. "We former students never get news of what's happening."

"We should put out a little magazine every once in a while," you say. "We could send it to all the graduates."

"I know a lot of them would want to read it," Mike says. "It should be easy to sell subscriptions, and you could get advertising money from local businesses."

The next day you go to talk to Mr. Dawkins about your new idea. You catch him in his office after class.

Go on to the next page.

"What would go in the magazine?" he asks.

"We could write about how our athletic teams are doing, give news about teachers and science projects—all kinds of things," you say.

Mr. Dawkins raps the table with his fist. "I like it. We could bring it out four times a year—call it the *Spring Rock Quarterly.* We can interview coaches, players, teachers, parents . . . ."

"I could ask a photography student to take pictures," you say. "And organize the team to sell advertising space around town."

Mr. Dawkins stands up and shakes your hand. "It's a great idea, and you thought it up," he says. "Would you like to be the quarterly's first student editor?"

"Sure," you say.

Turn to page 94.

You have butterflies in your stomach, but you're determined not to chicken out. This could be a big opportunity for the team, and Mr. Dawkins told you to show initiative, so you look up Coach Garafalo in the phone book and dial his number.

One ring . . . two rings:

"Hello," a voice says. "You have reached the Garafalo family. No one can come to the phone right now. If you'd like to leave a message, please do so when you hear the beep."

You think of hanging up, but that doesn't seem right, so you give your name and ask Coach Garafalo to call back—then you think you'd better add something else.

"You may not remember me," you say. "I played some at Windham and went to basketball camp. Well, I'm high scorer on the Spring Rock team now, and I don't know if you heard, but we have the best team in our history. I know we're two leagues below you, but I was wondering if there's any chance of our playing an exhibition game with Windham. Anyway, thanks."

You hang up. You always feel a little nervous leaving a long message on an answering machine—it's so easy to get tangled up with your words. And now you have to wait around, not knowing what Coach Garafalo will think of your call.

Go on to the next page.

You don't have to wait long. Within an hour, Garafalo calls back.

"Sure I remember you," he says. "And I heard that Spring Rock has a great team. It made me wish you were still at Windham!"

Turn to page 6.

On your way home, you split from Bob and Fred and stop by the 7-Eleven. Clive Wilson is waiting at the checkout counter. You've barely gotten to know Clive, though he's a real mover in your class. He catches your eye.

You say hi.

He hands the clerk some money and waits for change. He glances at you disdainfully. "What's up with you? Not much, I suppose."

Not much, I suppose. That's typical of this guy. He thinks he's so cool, so important. You feel like telling him who you just met. That would put him in his place. Clive would be so jealous he couldn't stand it.

You remember Jeffrey telling you to keep your meeting a secret. Still, you can't see what harm it would do to mention it to just one person.

If you decide to tell Clive about meeting Jeffrey Gordon, turn to page 89.

If you decide to keep quiet, turn to page 112.

FRESH
COFFEE
DIAPERS
DIAPERS
MILK
$2.59 GAL
EGGS
$1.29
CARS
DRINK
BASKETBALL
BLACK CAT
BLAC
Cola
2 LITRE
99¢

As the season goes on, Spring Rock wins game after game. The players' morale is high. Everyone gets a boost from being on a winning team. Despite this, you're not feeling happy. Coach Bartok must notice it, because one day he takes you aside after practice.

"I can tell something's bothering you," he says. "But I can't tell why. You're playing terrifically. We're headed for an undefeated season."

"That's part of what's bothering me," you say. "Suppose we do beat everyone. It wouldn't really mean anything—we're expected to. I wish we could play some teams in the A league—get a shot at the state championship."

"We couldn't compete on that level," Bartok says. "Spring Rock has always been in the C league. We may have a season or two when we're playing at B or maybe at times even on an A level, but it won't last."

Turn to page 10.

Your center does his job perfectly, standing strong and taking a hard shot from your defender as he collides with him. This allows you to make your move and drive to the hoop. The ball leaves your hand and finds the net just as a frustrated Lakesider swats your arm, drawing the foul. You make the foul shot to convert for the big three-point play!

Turn to page 75.

There's no chance of getting back to the fence, much less getting over it. Your only hope is the low-hanging branches of an apple tree near you. Not *so* low-hanging. You'll only have time for one leap, and you may not make it. But you don't think, you run—Bob and Fred running with you—and leap, hands outstretched, for the nearest branch. You grab it and swing your feet up, barely out of reach of the dogs barking and snapping at you from below. Glancing around, you see Bob on a lower branch, starting to climb higher. Fred is dangling from the next tree over, so low you're afraid the dog under him will pull him down.

You're about to call for help when you see that a sleek silver sedan has pulled up the drive. Two big men are getting out. One of them is Jeffrey Gordon! He claps his hands loudly.

"*Jam! Jive!* Get over here!"

The dogs bound toward him.

Jeffrey, patting the dogs, strolls over to the tree, his friend following. They're laughing as if they've just heard the world's funniest joke. Jeffrey looks up at you—he's so tall, he doesn't have to look far. "You can come down now. These dogs are trained not to bite, just to scare you to death."

Grateful, you drop to the ground.

Turn to page 9.

"Jeffrey," you say, "is there anything special we should remember? Like sort of your 'secrets of success'?"

He grins. "Okay, here are a few key things to remember:

"*One.* Be the best. Have total confidence in your game.

"*Two.* Compete not just to win but to *dominate.*" He eyes you a moment. "You want to be the best?"

"Sure," you say.

He nods. "Then make the hoop your life. Train hard. Practice hard, *always.* During game time have so much confidence that then you *relax,* and *dominate.*"

You start to say something, but Jeffrey holds up a finger. "Oh, and keep working on that vertical leap, and someday you'll jam the ball." He grins at you. "I'm not going to have time to meet with you again. I hope you'll all be a little better because of working out with me." He flicks his hand in a little wave. All that remains is for you to thank him and be on your way.

After missing the practice game, you know you won't get to see any action in the final game against Carthage. But you're sure you'll never regret it. You're determined to take Jeffrey's advice seriously. You have a feeling that it's going to make a difference for you in basketball, and in other things too.

Turn to page 105.

The next day after practice, you tell Coach Bartok about your conversation with Coach Garafalo. He looks rather startled.

"I think I'm the one who should have called Garafalo if anyone should have," he says.

"I'm sorry if I was out of line, but you didn't seem to think it would be possible," you say. "I thought with my connection to Windham, maybe it's a long shot, but why not give it a try? And you did say it would be nice if it could be arranged."

"Well, that's true," the coach says with a shrug. "But there are some things I'm worried about. Windham has a bigger, stronger team. They may just roll all over us. We're all so proud of our team at Spring Rock this year. It could really hurt morale."

"Coach, I know that everyone on our team would want to take that risk."

"Then there's the risk of injuries," he says.

"Our team may be a little smaller, but we're tough and we're in good shape," you say. "Besides, I know Coach Garafalo wouldn't let his players beat up on us even if they wanted to."

Coach Bartok stands back a step and squints at you. "You know," he says, "you're as good an arguer as you are a basketball player. Tell you what: I'll call Garafalo and discuss it with him."

Turn to page 71.

"You kids better move on," he says.

"This is a public road," Fred says.

"Not where you're standing. You're trespassing."

"Does Jeffrey Gordon's mother really live here?" you blurt out.

The guard looks slightly surprised. "Maybe so, maybe not."

"We know Jeffrey is visiting her," Fred says.

The guard reddens. He steps closer. "I don't care what you know," he says. "If you think you're getting anywhere near that house, or you're going to see Jeffrey Gordon, you're dead wrong."

"Hey, relax. We just want to get his autograph," you say.

"So do a million other people. Now keep off this property or I'll have the police chase you off." He struts off to his little guardhouse, leaving the three of you to decide what to do.

"We could just wait here," you say.

"The thing is," Bob says thoughtfully, "when Jeffrey arrives, he'll probably just turn in the drive, the guard will wave him on, and that's the last we'll see of him."

Fred puts a hand on each of your shoulders, as if you were in a football huddle. "Listen," he says. "Why don't we just slip around to the side and climb over the fence where the guard can't see us?"

Turn to page 82.

As you're heading back to the lockers, Coach Garafalo gives you a friendly pat on the back. "Tough game," he says.

"I'm disappointed how the year worked out for me," you say. "I was hoping I'd be able to touch the rim by now, but I guess it wasn't in the cards."

"It could be in the cards," Garafalo says. "You've got a lot of talent. I'd even say you're a natural. But you're young yet. You've got some growing to do. You need to put more into it—keep working on the basics and, most of all, develop more confidence in your game."

"How?"

"How?" He grins at you. "Well, for starters, I know a great basketball camp in Arizona. You could go there this summer. Work hard there and you won't be sitting on the bench next year."

Your talk with the coach gives you a lift, and you feel even better that evening when your parents okay the plan. Afterward, even though it's drizzling outside, you go out and shoot baskets, feeling like you just can't miss.

Turn to page 111.

32

You drive inside for the layup. A Lakeside player leaps to block you. You could take the foul, but instead of shooting you dribble once underneath and float a baby hook shot over his outstretched hand for two.

Lakeside takes the ball, the buzzer sounds, and you're into overtime. After a quick pep talk from the coach, you're centercourt again.

For most of the overtime, play is evenhanded. Both teams are patient and find ways to penetrate through the lane for easy layups. But with the clock running out, Windham gets a clean break off a rebound. You take a long pass from a teammate and drive down the court. The last couple of yards you're airborne like you've never been before. You watch as your hand brings the ball all the way to the hoop, jamming it for the final goal!

The stands go wild. Everyone is mobbing you, trying to get close, wanting to shake hands with the champ!

The End

DHAM
3
WIN
DHAI

"Well, thanks for saying that, Mr. Dawkins." You start to get up, but he motions for you to wait.

"Just a minute. I told you I didn't have a problem with your quitting the team, but I do have a problem with what you've been doing with yourself since then. Or I should say what you *haven't* been doing. You could be using the extra time to your advantage. But by all reports you've just been moping around, feeling sorry for yourself. Is that right?"

You shrug. "Maybe in some ways."

He nods. "Well, that's not very selfish. And I want you to be *selfish.*"

"Nobody ever told me to be selfish before," you say.

Mr. Dawkins holds up a finger. "Understand what I mean by that. I want you to think of what's best for you. In basketball, if you get knocked down, you pick yourself up off the floor and get back into the play, right? Well I want you to get back in control of your future. Remember what I said about doing something special?"

"Yes."

"Well *do* something. Now's your chance."

"How?"

Go on to the next page.

"Next month is the Windham County Science Fair. There is a category for high school entries, and you can win it. Think about what you've been studying. Find something you'd like to know more about, or *do* more about. That may give you a clue. Set up a project to find out more."

Turn to page 90.

The cop gets out of his car and strides toward you. "What are you kids up to?" he snaps.

But you're not looking at the cop. You're looking at the Jeffrey Gordon autograph on your new basketball, not a printed autograph but hand signed with a blue felt-tipped pen.

"Where did you get those balls?" the cop says.

"Presents from Mr. Jeffrey Gordon," you say. He glances at the security guard, who nods, looking almost as if a smile might appear on his face.

The cop takes a long look at the ball—you're holding it so he can see the autograph.

"Wish I had one of those," he says.

The End

Your pass is on the mark, and your teammate lines up the three-point shot. But just as he is about to shoot, the nearest Lakeside defender shouts. The sudden noise causes your teammate to flinch as he releases. The ball soars over its mark and into the hands of the Lakeside center.

Turn to page 75.

Fred replies, "Let's get as close as we can and still keep out of sight. When Jeffrey comes and gets out of his car, we'll just walk up and introduce ourselves."

"Yeah, maybe he'll invite us in for a Gatorade," you tease, punching Fred's arm.

"I could use one," Fred shoots back.

Bob spreads his hands, as if trying to block a pass. "Shhh! Keep your voices down!"

Keeping low, you move through the woods as close as you can to the house. At the edge of the lawn, you stop to gaze at the old apple trees and towering oaks.

"Let's get behind those shrubs," Fred says. "We'll be close to the drive and the house but still out of sight."

A minute more and you've staked out your new positions. Suddenly the front door opens. A woman wearing an apron—maybe a maid—looks out. You wonder if she can see you. She steps aside, and just about the biggest black dog you've ever seen slips past her. It lets out a single deep, loud bark and makes right for you. And there's another one behind it!

Turn to page 27.

You decide to transfer to Spring Rock. The school turns out to be smaller than you thought it would be, just a cluster of plain, white buildings on a hill. There are nice grounds and lots of big old trees, though, and a fairly new gym.

As you hoped, you don't have much trouble making the varsity basketball team. Right from the beginning you hold your own with the biggest and most experienced players. And in the first game Coach Bartok puts you in the starting lineup.

As your dad said, the coach is pretty good. The team steadily improves, and Spring Rock has its best season in years. The only trouble is that, being so small, the school is only rated C league. And because of budget cuts, C league teams no longer compete for the state championship.

That's a bummer, but of course you didn't come to Spring Rock just for basketball—you were also determined to perform well in the science program. Now that your first year there is winding up, you have to decide which branch of science you want to specialize in. You're torn between your two interests, space science and computer science, but now that your general science classes are over, you have to make a choice.

Decide now whether you want to register for the space science or the computer science program. Then, WHICHEVER YOU DECIDE, *turn to page 104.*

You launch the canoe again just below the rapids. There are more rapids ahead, but you have no trouble handling them. An hour and a half later you beach the canoe at the pickup spot. The van from the lodge is waiting.

"That was great," Jenny says as you load the canoe on top of the van.

"I wish we could sign up for another trip like this," Bass says.

"They only let you take one," Jenny says. "The rest is basketball, basketball, basketball."

She's right.

Turn to page 68.

Mr. Dawkins rises from his chair. He's not much taller than you are. His voice mimics you. "*I don't know if I can!* Is that the kind of thinking that made you Spring Rock's star basketball player?"

"No."

"Then think about it." He holds out his hand. The interview is over.

You leave feeling somewhat encouraged but also anxious. That night you lie awake a long time trying to come up with an inspiration. But you fall asleep before any ideas come to you.

Turn to page 24.

You slow down to ready yourself, then come in for the layup, your eyes fixed on the hoop. Out of nowhere the Windham center chases you down and blocks your shot, fouling you hard in the process. The foul leaves you with a stinging pain in your right shoulder.

Your first foul shot misses to the right. Maybe you favored your shoulder. Can't let that happen again.

You take a deep breath, bounce the ball a few times, cock your arm, and shoot. The ball hits the left side of the rim and bounces off. 0 for 2.

Turn to page 17.

"I bet Jeffrey bought it for her," you say.

"I'm sure he did," Bob says. "You know how much he's made from advertising endorsements?"

"Millions," you say.

"Megamillions," Fred says. He holds out his wrist so you can see his watch. "It's quite a ways out there—we'd better get going."

Bob answers by hopping on his bike and racing down the drive. Fred follows, with you right behind him.

About half an hour later the three of you are chugging up Sequoia Road. You haven't been out this way in a long time and you'd forgotten what it's like. Big houses with tremendous lawns. Great old trees. Most of the houses are set quite far back. You can only catch glimpses of them through the trees.

You reach a property with a wrought iron fence running along the front. Bob comes to a stop and gets off his bike. You and Fred do the same.

"This is the place," Bob says. "Sixty-one Sequoia Road."

The fence is about seven feet high, with spikes on top sticking up even higher. Beyond it is a dense stand of hemlocks. You try to peer through them. "Where's the house?"

"Back in there." Bob points to the driveway entrance up ahead, blocked by an iron gate. A tiny building stands next to it. A uniformed guard comes out and starts toward you.

Turn to page 30.

You close in on the defender at the foul line. He lunges toward you, arms outstretched. You try to pass to the right, but his timing is perfect. He gets a hand on the ball and knocks it away. One of your teammates comes up with the loose ball in three-point land, but his back's to the net. He wheels with only one second left and fires up a prayer. The prayer goes unanswered. Time runs out, and Windham loses by a single point.

Turn to page 31.

During the final week of camp you spend time with weights, stretching, sprints, and running. Every day you strengthen your muscles and improve your vertical stretch more with Coach Rice's help. Results come quickly, and by the time camp's over you can almost touch the rim.

You return home a better player than when you left—no doubt about that. But you still have doubts as to whether you can ever be a standout at Windham. That's why you're kind of interested when your parents tell you about an opportunity you might want to consider. There's a private school called Spring Rock on the other side of town. Students come there from all over the country.

"There are two reasons you might like to transfer there," your dad tells you. "One is that they have a very good science program. You've done well in your science courses at Windham and if you continued to do well at Spring Rock, it could really be a help when you apply for college. Second, since it's a small school, I figure you'd have no trouble making the basketball team. In fact you'd probably be a starter. I know you really want to play this year. And I hear they have a very good coach."

"I think it would be a good move," your mom says. "Of course, the decision is up to you."

If you decide to transfer to Spring Rock, turn to page 40.

If you decide to stay at Windham, turn to page 105.

The guard comes out, motions them to drive in, and starts back toward his guardhouse.

The three of you race forward, yelling. "Hey, Jeffrey! Welcome to Windham! Can we get your autograph?"

You're only a few feet from Jeffrey's car as it turns into the drive. It stops for a moment while the gate opens. You and your friends keep running toward it. The guard whips his big frame around, blocking Bob and Fred, but you throw a body fake right, pivot with your left foot, and slip past his outstretched palm.

"Smooth move, champ," Jeffrey calls out to you through his open window.

"I learned it from watching you," you call back. "Can we get your autograph, Mr. Gordon?" But Jeffrey has turned to say something to the man next to him.

The gate opens, and the car starts though. But out of the sunroof, lofting like a game-winning three-pointer, comes a basketball—then a second, then a third! You catch the first one. Bob and Fred scramble for the others.

By now the gate has closed behind Jeffrey's sedan. A police car is pulling up. The guard is standing in front of the gate, his arms crossed, a mean look on his face.

Turn to page 37.

There is plenty of scoring on both sides. Spring Rock is gaining. Time goes by quickly and suddenly, all too suddenly, there's less than a minute to play. Windham is up by only two points, and they've got the ball, nursing it, feeding it around the perimeter, killing time.

The shot clock is ticking. A Spring Rock player tries desperately to steal a pass, misses, goes off balance, opening a Windham forward to receive the ball. He gets it. Drives in. A Spring Rock player races to guard him. Twenty seconds left.

Windham has a player open at the post. You guess he's going to get a pass, and you leap for it and knock it away, barely keeping your balance, trying to control the ball. But the Windham center slaps a big hand on it and reels it in. A second later he shoots. Misses!

Again you leap, this time batting the ball down in front of you, getting control, letting your momentum carry you as you speed-dribble down the court, eye on the clock. Ten seconds . . . nine . . . eight. Two Windham players are streaking to cut you off. You pass to a forward. He can't shoot. He bounce passes back to you. Your path is blocked; you curl out beyond the three-point line.

Go on to the next page.

Four seconds left. A Windham player is racing to guard you. Your forward is free now, in the corner. Should you shoot? Or rifle a pass to him?

If you shoot, turn to page 63.

If you pass to your forward, turn to page 87.

You call Fred when you get home. "Count me in!" you tell him.

"Great," he says. "Be here by ten-thirty Saturday."

That Saturday morning you bike over to Fred's house, determined to have Jeffrey Gordon's autograph before the day is through. You show up around ten-thirty, just as Fred told you to. Bob Rosewald is already there. He's

such a tall guy you're surprised he didn't make the squad.

Fred is wearing a backpack. "I brought some drinks and corn chips," he says. "We may have to hang out there awhile, but I'm sure if we wait long enough we'll see Jeffrey."

"How do you know all this?" you ask.

Go on to the next page.

Fred points to Bob, who looks around as if to make sure no one's listening—though since you're all standing halfway down his driveway, you don't see how anyone could be. "Don't let on," he says. "My mom is a friend of the real estate broker who handled the purchase of the house. She told Mom that Jeffrey's mother moved here to be near her father, Jeffrey's granddad. He's real old—he's in the Crestview Nursing Home. You know, the one out on Route 6."

"Got you," you say. "So where is this house she bought, anyway?"

"Sequoia Road."

Fred shoots you a glance. "She must be rich."

Turn to page 45.

After about ten minutes of hard play, the three of you are pretty winded. Not Jeffrey: he's still moving as quickly as a cat after a mouse, shifting direction without missing a step—as if it's no effort at all. Sometimes he just seems to float around you, while your shoes feel nailed to the floor.

After a while he invites you to sit down at an outdoor table. A maid brings juice and soda.

"I've tried to give you a few tips today," Jeffrey says. "I hope they're helpful, but they're just the beginning, and unfortunately you can't rely on me as a teacher." He gets up from his chair. He's too polite to say so, but you can tell that the clinic is over.

Turn to page 28.

You show up for the practice game. Your performance improves but not enough to get you off the bench the following Saturday in the big game with Carthage. At least not until Windham's first-string point guard fouls out late in the fourth quarter. You feel a little jolt of adrenaline when the coach motions to you.

The game is very tight when you go out on the court. The pace is intense. Each team has a couple of turnovers, and you don't even get your hands on the ball. With only forty-five seconds left, Carthage has the lead by two, and one of your teammates is heading up the court with the ball. He drives to the foul line where he is double-teamed, leaving you wide open.

He passes to you just as your defender drops away. You catch the ball, move inside, and dish a bounce pass between the legs of an oncoming defender to your waiting center. He sinks a quick three-foot jumper to tie the score.

Only twenty seconds left. Coach Garafalo motions for a full-court press in hopes of getting a steal. But your man has the ball and is able to keep it away from you simply by backing down the court with his body shielding you from the ball. With twelve seconds left, you decide to foul him and hope for a missed foul shot—this will stop the clock and should give Windham the ball again with enough time for the final shot. The next time he backs into you, you push his elbow. The ref blows his whistle. The clock stops, and the Carthage player goes to the line.

Turn to page 76.

CARTHAGE
:14
WINDHAM
52
52
EXIT

The next day you quit the basketball team and go out for winter track. You're never going to be a track star, but at least it gets your mind off things.

And there are a lot of things you want to get your mind off. Like how not just the coach but a lot of others seem to feel you let them down by quitting the team. And how maybe it's going to make it harder for you to get good recommendations when you apply to college.

One day Mr. Dawkins passes you in the hall and asks you to stop into his office. You don't feel like it—you're sure he's just going to scold you for quitting basketball—but there's no avoiding it.

You're surprised, when you sit down, to see him looking at you sympathetically. "I've heard rumors," he says. "But I'd like you to tell me personally. Why did you quit the team?"

You tell him everything that happened. He makes notes on a yellow pad.

"I guess you're going to tell me I messed up," you say.

"No, I'm not," he says. "I'll let you be the judge of that. You have a right to quit if you want to. Perhaps you should have been more diplomatic and told Coach Bartok about the phone call you made. Then he wouldn't have felt you were ignoring him. On the other hand, your idea was a good one. And he shouldn't have squashed it just because it wasn't his."

Turn to page 34.

"Keep your eyes out for a big sign on the left that says PORTAGE. Pull out there and carry your canoe along the trail. It's a quarter of a mile, and you have to climb partway, but it's worth it. Then you reenter the river below the rapids and continue on from there. It sounds like more work than it is. You've got a light canoe, and you're all in good shape from camp, right?"

You all nod.

He raises a hand and gives a military salute. "Okay then, be careful and have fun."

You launch the canoe, getting in the bow, with Jenny in the middle and Bass in the stern. Bass pushes off, and you're on your way.

Go on to the next page.

You slowly paddle down the river, the current taking you briskly along. Strange and beautiful rock formations—looking red, orange, or pink depending on how the light hits them—pass by on either side. Scraggly trees grow out of the cracks in the canyon walls. Cliff swallows dart in and out of their nests.

Sometimes you pass through white water, little choppy wavelets. Nothing you can't handle, but enough to make you and Bass stroke vigorously to weave your way around the rocks.

Hours pass. The sun beats down on you. You take off your life jackets.

Turn to page 67.

62

The next morning you, Bob, and Fred bike up to 61 Sequoia Road, arriving a little before noon. You're surprised to see another security guard in addition to the one you saw the day before. You pull up next to the driveway entrance and get off your bikes. Both men start toward you.

"Jeffrey's expecting us," you say. "He told us—"

"He's *not* expecting you," the new guard says. "*No* visitors."

"That can't be," Bob says angrily. "He said—"

The other guard cuts in. "Whatever he said was before a couple of dozen people showed up here. We've had cars stopping here all morning, people trying to see Mr. Gordon."

"But he said he would see us," you insist.

"That was before you spread the news all over town!"

"We didn't spread it all over town."

"I didn't tell anyone," Bob says.

"I didn't," Fred echoes.

"I only told Clive Wilson," you say.

Fred stamps his foot on the ground and throws down his bike. "Clive Wilson? That's the same as spreading it all over town."

It's obvious he's right, and there's nothing you can do about it now. You blew your chance to play in the final game of the season. And now you've blown your chance to get coached by Jeffrey Gordon!

The End

You jump shoot for the three-pointer. The Windham center panics and hits your arm. The ball goes wild. The whistle blows. You have three free throws with the clock frozen at four seconds to play. If you sink two of them, the game goes into overtime; sink three and Spring Rock has won!

A hush falls over the stands. All eyes are on you. You take a deep breath, cock your arm, and push the ball up in a perfect arc—*swoosh* through the hoop. You try to do the same with your second throw. It brushes the rim, spins, and spills over. No point. Your final throw brushes the inside of the rim, spins, and falls through to tie the score.

A Windham player takes the ball out and then hurls a long overhead pass that hits the top of the backboard and falls harmlessly into the arms of the other Spring Rock guard.

Into overtime.

Two turnovers for each team. Missed shots, missed passes, as if everyone is exhausted. Which is true.

With seconds left, a teammate bounces the ball to you.

Turn to page 98.

You cock your arm and let the ball slide off and up in a graceful arc. Everything seems to go in slow motion as you watch the ball sail over the hoop. It hits the backboard, comes down on the rim, and bounces into the hands of the leaping Lakeside center. He fakes with his foot, then rifles a pass to a teammate in midcourt as the final buzzer sounds.

People are patting you on the back. "Good game." Sure. "You played real well, even if you did miss that final attempt." Sure, thanks. But what difference does it make? Your team lost, 65–63.

Coach Garafalo comes up. You're almost afraid to face him after missing that final shot.

"I should have driven in for the layup," you tell him. "It's so obvious. Sent us into overtime."

"What do you mean 'obvious'?" he says. "You might not have gotten in for the layup. And if you had, you probably would have been fouled, gotten two free throws, and if you hadn't made both of them, we'd still have lost. You have to use your gut instinct in a situation like that, and I'm not going to say yours was wrong."

"I still feel I didn't think straight."

"No time to think on court—it's got to be automatic," he says. "That's what experience is. That's what you need. And you're going to get plenty of it. I happen to know." He winks and turns to talk to another player, leaving you wondering what he meant.

Turn to page 117.

65
63
INDHAM
7
NDHAM
3

It's an eighteen-mile course through some beautiful gorges. The idea is to land the canoe and have a picnic lunch along the way. A van from the lodge will pick you up downstream and bring you back.

You get your supplies and a map, and you're ready to push off. The guide at the lodge checks out your equipment, reviews basic safety procedures, and makes sure your life jackets are fastened securely.

"Any of you have white-water experience?" he asks.

"I have, back East," Bass says.

"I've just done lake canoeing," Jenny says.

You tell what you've done.

"Basically this is a routine run," the guide says. "Just keep your canoe right side up. You'll see a big sign where you're to get out that says HIGH POINT CANOES LAND HERE. That's where we'll pick you up in the van."

"Can't make a wrong turn," Jenny says. "The river only runs one way."

The guide returns a thin smile. "I said that *basically* it's routine. But the river has been running high, so be on your guard. There's a very rough stretch—number-five water we call it—about two-thirds of the way down that you won't want to mess with.

Turn to page 59.

"This is really great," Jenny says.

"Better than basketball camp," Bass says.

"It's making me hungry," you say. "Let's keep an eye out for a good place to land."

"How about that flat grassy area up ahead on the left?" Jenny says, pointing. "Where the sign is."

"Portage," you say, reading it.

"Oh, we're supposed to land there anyway," Jenny says.

"Hey, let's go through the white water first. We can make it," Bass says.

You look around at him and catch the anxious look on Jenny's face.

"Do you think it's all right?" she says.

If you say, "I think we can handle it," turn to page 93.

If you say, "I think it's too risky," turn to page 101.

During the next couple of weeks at basketball camp you really give it all you've got. You listen to your coaches and ask questions about offensive and defensive strategy, and with two, sometimes three, practice games a day you have ample opportunity to try things out. You even stay late after evening games and shoot baskets after everyone else has gone. Sometimes, when no one else is around, you leap at the basket and try to jam the ball, but you never come close.

You get so that all you think about is basketball. And when you play, there's a little computer in your head calculating how good the chances are of any move you might make.

One day a coach named Stan Rice takes you aside. He coaches a high school in Texas and speaks with that soft, easygoing Texan voice.

"I've been watching you out there. You've got a lot of heart and some natural ability. You can do a lot of things pretty well," he tells you. "But what skill would you most like to develop?"

You chuckle. "I guess the one that I *can't* develop."

"What would that be?"

Go on to page 70.

"I'd like to be able to jam the ball," you say.

"Who says you can't develop that? I personally know a guy who can dunk and he's only five feet six," the coach says. "And I know another guy who's six-four and can't even get his fingers on the rim. As for you, you're young—you've got to grow a little—but I've seen you leap pretty high, and I bet you haven't even been working at it."

"I try almost every day," you protest.

"Sure you do. On the court. But it takes more than that. It takes strength training." He points to your legs. "We've got to put springs in those legs."

Turn to page 47.

Three weeks have passed. The game with Windham is on! They had an open date in their schedule, and Spring Rock could rearrange its own schedule to make room for it.

Needless to say, everyone at Spring Rock is hyped up for the game. The team is practicing harder than ever. Every ticket is sold out. They're even going to broadcast the game on local television.

Saturday before the big game, you and your family go to watch Windham play a regular league game. The Windham players are big, fast, and accurate shooters. They win by fifteen points. After the game, you hear a couple of guys—Windham fans—talking behind you.

"Windham is going to win the state championship. You can quote me."

"They might even beat mighty Spring Rock next Saturday."

The first guy lets out a big guffaw. "Yeah, Spring Rock. That's a good one. The Spring Rock team will be sorry they ever came out of their playpen!"

You feel like saying something to this loudmouth but decide to save your energy for the game.

Turn to page 92.

You think about what Mr. Dawkins told you, and you come up with an idea for a space science project. Your idea is to make a model of the sun and the twenty-five nearest stars—showing just where they are in space.

It's not easy. You have to go to three libraries before you find a star atlas that shows the direction, distance, diameter, and color of each of the twenty-five nearest stars. Since the farthest of them is 13.4 light-years away, you decide to use a scale of two inches per light-year. Your model will then be about four and a half feet across.

You get permission to hang the model from the ceiling at the main entrance hall of the school while you work on it. For the sun, you hang a bright yellow bead from a fine piece of thread. Then you hang blue, red, and yellow beads, each of which represents a star—larger beads for the larger stars and smaller beads for the smaller ones. When you're finished, you have a three-dimensional model that shows just how far and in what direction each star is from the sun, plus its color and its size compared to the sun. The model shows the view you would have from a spacecraft traveling through our part of the galaxy.

A picture of your model appears in the local newspaper. After the county competition, you're invited to install it at the local planetarium!

Turn to page 13.

"Yeah, but right now second-string," you say.

Jeffrey and his friend exchange glances. "Second-string?" He feigns a look of surprise. "Well, maybe I can help you. I'll be here for a few days. Come back about this time tomorrow—we'll have a little clinic. See if we can do something about your game. Just don't tell anyone you met me, okay?"

"We won't," you all say, shaking your heads.

Jeffrey motions to his friend, who tosses him a cellular phone. He starts dialing a number. "See ya—the guard will let you out." He turns and starts toward the house, talking into the phone.

The three of you walk down the drive, half exultant, half keeping an eye on the dogs. They stand motionless, eyes fixed on you, as if daring you to come back. But you don't mind them. You have an appointment for a basketball lesson with maybe the greatest player who ever lived.

Turn to page 22.

In the fourth quarter, Lakeside comes to life. Windham has led the whole game, but some careless turnovers combined with great Lakeside passing whittle away your lead. You watch in disbelief as a simple pick-and-roll puts Lakeside over the top! Coach Garafalo smacks his fist in his palm and jumps up and down. You can't hear what he's saying over the cheering of the crowd, but you know it isn't nice.

From then on it's a tight back-and-forth battle, with Lakeside holding the edge. You are so caught up in the game that when you finally think to check the scoreboard, there are just two minutes left to play! Lakeside 64, Windham 60, and Lakeside has the ball.

Their center, tightly guarded up above the key, passes along the perimeter and immediately gets the ball back. Another pass. Back again. Using up time. The shot clock's running. The Lakeside center tosses the ball to the wing and races forward, looking for the give-and-go as he reaches the post.

Turn to page 79.

The pressure is on him now. He bounces the ball twice and, without a hint of fear, shoots his first free throw. Nothing but net.

Your stomach drops as you think about the possibility of Windham losing because of your foul. You hope he misses the second shot, but Windham's got to be ready to rebound and score in ten seconds.

Again he steps up to the line. He bounces the ball twice and takes the shot, but this time he's just off the mark. The ball glances off the rim, and your center comes down strong with the rebound. There's still hope.

The clock is ticking, and Windham is out of time-outs. You're downcourt in a hurry. The center makes a beautiful long pass to you at the top of the key, and you find yourself in a three-on-two situation in your favor. You dribble hard toward the basket. The two Carthage defenders are in your way with their backs to the net. You're heading toward them at full speed with one teammate on your left and one on your right. Your plan is to draw a Carthage defender to you and pass to the open man for an easy layup and the win.

Turn to page 46.

You decide to wait where you are and hope for rescue.

Hours pass. They feel like days. You call out for help, but there is no reply, only the incessant roar of the white water. Hunched on the narrow rock, you endure the cold waves splashing up at your legs.

The sun sinks beneath the rim of the canyon. The river waters turn a grayish black. The shoreline becomes indistinct. The twilight wanes. You shiver, soaked, exhausted, huddling in the damp chill of the early evening air.

Then you hear a noise overhead—a helicopter! You haven't been forgotten. A searchlight casts a swath of light along the shore. You stand up and wave, but you're stiff from crouching so long. One of your feet goes out from under you. You claw desperately for a grip as your hip falls hard onto the rock and you slide into the dark, swirling waters.

Drained, like the ball dropping through the hoop.

Seconds later the current smashes you hard into a boulder, and you let yourself go. Your last game is over.

The End

LAKESIDE
5
WINDHAM
3
LAKESIDE
11
77
10

You're looking too. You leap at just the right moment and pick the ball out of the air, then dribble half the court before rifling it to a teammate in the wing.

A hustling Lakeside player blocks his lane, but he shoots anyway, *swoosh,* for three, an amazing shot under pressure. Lakeside 64, Windham 63.

Now Lakeside drives down the court, with less than a minute to play.

A Windham player guarding the ball handler commits too early. The Lakeside forward darts around him. He's fouled—two free throws for Lakeside. They sink one, then miss the second.

Twenty-three seconds: Lakeside 65, Windham 63, and your other guard has it, taking it up court. A Windham forward is free in the post. But the pass to him is cut off. The Lakeside player bobbles it. Loose ball. Your forward recovers but defenders swarm his shot. He dishes it to your waiting hands. You check your feet. You're good for three, if you make it. Four seconds, now three.

If you shoot for the game-winning three-pointer, turn to page 64.

If you drive in for the layup, turn to page 32.

Your spirits sink even further when he shakes his head while going through your folder. When he finally looks up, he smiles, but that doesn't make you feel any better.

"What are your plans for when you graduate, young man?"

"I plan to attend college," you say, "and get a degree in science."

"How are you set financially?"

"I'll need some help. My dad tells me I need to get a scholarship."

"Scholarships are for outstanding students, you know." Mr. Dawkins looks you in the eye.

"Yes, I know. It doesn't look good, does it?"

"I didn't say that. I'm just saying you need to stand out. I think you'll have to do something extra special this year to call attention to yourself."

"You mean extracurricular activities—like working on the school paper or joining the drama club?"

"That's not special enough," he says. "Think not just about *joining* something, but about *starting* something: *breaking new ground.* For example, last year a senior, Marie Pizarro, started *The Griffin,* the school magazine that publishes poems and stories written by students. You've seen it, haven't you?"

Go on to the next page.

"Sure, but that sort of thing doesn't interest me much."

"I'm not saying it should," Mr. Dawkins says. "But it's an example of how a student didn't just *join* an organization, but *started* one. Not that I'm saying you have to start an organization. I just mean you should try to do something that hasn't been done before. Be creative. Follow?"

"Sure," you say. "But I don't know if I can."

Turn to page 43.

"We'll hide out near the house until Jeffrey comes," Fred continues, "and then try to get his autograph."

"And maybe get arrested," Bob says.

"He's not going to arrest some kids, especially ones who are big fans of his," Fred says. He looks at you. "How about it? Are you game?"

You *feel* game, but something tells you that you need to think this through more.

If you say, "Let's just wait here," turn to page 14.

If you say, "Let's try to sneak in," turn to page 109.

Bartok gives you a pat on the back. "I can see you're disappointed. Next time check with me before making any big calls like that."

The bell for the next class rings. He starts to add something, but you just say, "Gotta go," and hurry off to class.

You don't have much spirit for basketball practice that afternoon. The coach must notice it, but he doesn't say anything. He knows you're feeling bad, probably thinks you'll get over it. But you have a feeling you *won't* get over it. In fact, you have a good mind to quit the team. Maybe you'll work harder in your courses, try to get better marks. You have three science courses in your specialization unit and that's a lot of work. There wasn't much hope of getting a basketball scholarship anyway.

If you decide to quit the team, turn to page 58.

If you decide to stick it out, turn to page 91.

"There's a rock to the left!" Bass shouts. "Gotta get around it!"

"We'll go broadside!"

Then—so fast you don't see it coming—the canoe strikes a rock, hanging up the bow. The current whips the stern violently around. Suddenly you're capsized, swimming, gasping for air, whipped by violent waves. You've lost your grip on the canoe, the paddle, everything.

There's a rock ahead of you, barely out of the water, right in midstream. The current carries you swiftly toward it. Reaching it, you grab hold and with a terrific effort heave yourself up. You crouch there, shivering and exhausted, slapped by an endless succession of waves.

Your friends are nowhere in sight. Neither is the canoe.

There are a few spots along the shore where they may have been able to pull themselves up. If they haven't, the current will have taken them around the next bend by now, and the canoe, too, if it hasn't broken up.

From what you can see, you're through the worst of the rapids, but you can't be sure. What should you do? Crouch here on this spray-soaked rock, or jump in and try to reach calmer waters? If you stay here long enough, the waves splashing on you will chill you to the bone. On the other hand, once you jump in, you'll be at the mercy of the river.

If you swim for it, turn to page 100.

If you stick where you are, turn to page 77.

Reading through some computer magazines in your school library, you come up with a great idea for a computer science project for the upcoming science fair. Your idea is to make a computer simulation of a freshwater pond. To do this you take photos of a nearby pond, a little boat, and some ducks. You scan them in to the computer, then scan in pictures of tiny creatures that might be found in the pond.

You draw some other things on your graphics program and design your software so that someone playing it on a computer can move the boat around and see various things up close.

The player will also have a "microscope." He or she will be able to hold it over a duck's feathers, click on it, and see the finest detail, right down to individual cells. Or click on part of the pond and see microscopic creatures in a drop of water, and even bacteria inside them! Then click again and see molecules inside the bacteria, and even individual atoms!

Turn to page 13.

You pass to your teammate on the wing. Rushed by the clock, he panics, calls time-out when you don't have one. Windham's ball. They hold it for the remaining seconds. Game over.

What a letdown—so close and then to lose. The Windham fans are all cheering. But so are the Spring Rock fans—it was such a great effort. Everyone is congratulating everyone else, especially you. The Windham coach, the principal, and the mayor all tell you what an exciting game it was, how well you played, how you really put Spring Rock on the map.

A familiar figure squeezes through the crowd, like a dribbler weaving through defenders. It's Mr. Dawkins. He reaches over and shakes your hand.

"That was something special you did, setting up this game," he says. "And your playing was something special too." He gives you a thumbs-up sign. "You're going places. I'll stake my reputation on it."

The End

You'd definitely do it, except you don't want to make a fool of yourself. Besides, if it got back to Coach Bartok that you called Garafalo, he might think you were cutting in on his job. He might get pretty sore at you. That's the last thing you want—you'll be needing his recommendation for your college application.

If you decide to call Coach Garafalo and try to set up an exhibition game, turn to page 20.

If you decide not to call him, turn to page 18.

"You know Bob Rosewald and Fred Stauffer?" you say. "The three of us just met with Jeffrey Gordon."

Clive picks up his change and a package. He looks at you skeptically. "*The* Jeffrey Gordon?"

"That's who I mean."

"Why're you giving me a line like that?"

"I'm not kidding," you say. "Jeffrey's mother moved to Windham because her father is in a nursing home here. Jeffrey came to help her get settled."

You and Clive begin ambling toward the exit. "So how did you meet him?"

You're not so sure you should tell about climbing over the fence, so you say, "We just hung out there and waited till he drove up."

By now you and Clive are outside. You unlock your bike and start to get on it. "Well, see you," you say.

"Hey, wait a minute." Clive is practically blocking your way. "Jeffrey Gordon! That's cool. Where's the house?"

"Up on Sequoia Road."

"Figures," Clive says. "That's something. What did he say?"

Clive is really impressed—no doubt of that. But you're beginning to feel you shouldn't have started blabbing. "Got to go," you say, and push off on your bike.

Turn to page 62.

The bell sounds. It's time for class. You thank Mr. Dawkins for his advice and walk out of his office feeling a little confused. At least it was nice to have someone say it was all right for you to quit the team.

If, earlier, you decided to specialize in computer science, turn to page 86.

If you decided to specialize in space science, turn to page 73.

You decide not to quit the team. Might as well stick at it and do your best, you think.

That kind of thinking pays off. With you as its spark plug, Spring Rock goes on to its second undefeated season in a row.

Soon after the season ends, you find yourself in Mr. Dawkins's office again.

He sits across from you at his desk, looking over your records while you wait nervously, wondering what he's going to say.

"I guess I didn't do anything special, the way you suggested," you say.

"No, but your marks have improved, and your involvement with basketball should help," he says. "You have a shot at getting a scholarship."

"Just a shot?"

"Just a shot," he says. "As if it were overtime in a basketball game, with the score tied and time running out. You're driving down the court. No time to pass, you've got to shoot from way out."

"That's called a low percentage shot," you say. "Means I probably won't make it."

"You've made a lot of shots like that on the court these past couple of years. You never stopped to think about how you might miss."

"Yes, but this is like the last game of the season—this is the championship. If I don't make this shot I'm through."

Turn to page 116.

The big day arrives. You're on the court, the stands packed on both sides, video cameras trained on the action. It's like living a dream, hard to believe it's actually happening! You imagine yourself playing on prime time TV for the NBA play-offs.

You warm up, shoot around, getting in the groove. You lose track of time. Suddenly it's the tip-off. The opening minutes will be crucial in setting the tone for the game. Will Windham intimidate your squad early on or will Spring Rock rally and gain confidence? The ball goes up and the Windham center bats the toss to his forward, who drives in, fakes outside, and lays it in with ease. Windham 2, Spring Rock 0.

You take the ball inbounds. You hurl a long outlet pass to your forward, but Windham covers against the fast break. Spring Rock moves the ball around but can't get a player free in the post.

The ball comes to you again. Your shooting guard is free. You bounce pass to him and he shoots a flat ten-footer. The ball hits the rim, Windham grabs the rebound, quickly brings it up court, and their guard finishes it with another easy layup. Windham 4, Spring Rock 0.

Turn to page 103.

"I think we can handle it," you say.

Jenny still looks anxious. "I don't know about this," she says.

"Look," Bass says. "We can all swim. We'll put our life jackets back on. The worst that can happen is we'll tip over and get wet. Come on—this is the real fun."

"Okay," Jenny says, "but let's *not* tip over."

You all put your life jackets back on. Then Bass paddles vigorously past the PORTAGE sign and on downstream. The canoe rounds a bend. The riverbank is replaced by sheer cliffs rising on either side. Flecks of white lie on the water ahead.

You hear a roar from around the next bend.

"Is that a waterfall?" Jenny shouts. You can hear the panic in her voice.

"Just the rapids—number-five water!" Bass yells back. He breaks off, suddenly paddling hard to avoid a rock. The current sweeps the canoe off course. You paddle furiously to get it headed downstream again. Suddenly there are rocks ahead, breaking the surface, sending up water and spray.

The canoe plunges down a wave. You stroke with all your might to keep it from going broadside. Ahead steep, crazy waves rise everywhere. Suddenly you're in them, you and Bass struggling to keep the canoe from tipping.

A sheer drop ahead. "Go left!" you yell.

Turn to page 84.

94

The first issue of the Spring Rock quarterly, *The Rocker,* comes out late that spring. The basketball team's undefeated season is the cover story. A few days afterward Mr. Dawkins calls you into his office. Smiling, he says, "I've got good news for you. You've been chosen for the Alumni Award for making an outstanding contribution to the school. You get a plaque with it and—oh yes—one thousand dollars in scholarship money. Congratulations."

"Gee, thanks."

"Don't thank me, I didn't have anything to do with it," he says. "It was the Awards Committee—they liked the way you did something special. Not that I don't think you deserved it. Next year, whenever I'm trying to encourage a student, you're going to be my star example!"

The End

THE
ROCKER
IT'S QUARTERLY
CAGERS UNDEFEATED
MISS WHIGMORE IS TEACHER OF THE MONTH
JAMAAL ELECTED PRESIDENT
SMITHSON WINS VICE PREZ!!!

Spring Rock hangs in there admirably, but the size and strength of Windham's players begin to seem like too much of an advantage to overcome. At the half it's Windham 27, Spring Rock 18.

Back in the locker room, Coach Bartok stands on a bench, sweating as if he'd been running up and down the court with you. "We've proven we can play in the same league with these guys," he says. "Congratulations. Now let's go one step further and show we can beat them! Right now they must be feeling pretty confident. They may let up a little. But we're not going to let up. I want every one of you to go for broke. Make them work harder than they're willing to work. I want to see everyone crashing the boards. Set your picks, screens, and cuts the way we've drilled day in and day out. This game belongs to you!"

You've never heard Coach Bartok so inspired.

Out on the court again. Furious pace. The fouls mount up. The crowd gets noisier, screaming and yelling on both sides.

Some wild shots, and some great ones. And Spring Rock is gaining! Going into the last quarter, it's Windham 43, Spring Rock 38.

As the fourth quarter gets underway, you drive hard to the hoop, laying the ball in twice, scoring once from three-point land, stealing the ball, getting stripped yourself, then running down your opponent, taking a rebound, and rifling it down to a forward who lays it in.

Turn to page 50.

"Just tell the coach you can't make it—he'll still let you play."

You laugh when you hear this. "No way, Fred. The coach sounds as if he's ready to throw me off the team as it is. I've got no chance at all if I don't show up at that practice game."

"Suit yourself, but let me know if you change your mind."

The bus is about to leave. You give Fred a quick good-bye and step on board. You sit by the window, watching the traffic, thinking. You have a chance to meet Jeffrey Gordon. And what's the point of blowing it just so you can knock yourself out trying to satisfy Coach Garafalo? If you did meet Jeffrey, maybe some of his greatness would rub off on you. Maybe he could teach you more than you'd ever learn from the coach.

You decide to call Fred the moment you get home and tell him to count you in. But then another thought crosses your mind. Jeffrey Gordon would probably tell you it was more important to show up for the practice game.

All this thinking isn't helping you decide. But decide you must—Saturday is coming up fast.

If you decide to show up for the practice game, turn to page 56.

If you decide to hang out with Fred and Bob and see if you can meet Jeffrey Gordon, turn to page 52.

You drive down the court, split two defenders with a stutter step, and reach the post before being guarded. Pass to your teammate on wing. He dribbles, pivots, back to you. Tightly guarded, you start to jump as if to shoot, then, with a crossover dribble, drive in. You're blocked again. Not quite. There's an open lane, but you've got to move and you've got to take it all the way in. No time to think about percentages; you palm the ball in one hand, take two giant steps and a soaring leap, and in one fluid motion, *jam it home!*

A second later the buzzer blasts. Spring Rock 67, Windham 65!

The Spring Rock fans go wild. You're hugging teammates, getting tossed in the air, then trying to get through the mob. No way. The floor is mobbed. Cops and teachers look on helplessly as Spring Rock fans cut down the nets. Coach Bartok makes it through to shake your hand. His head is soaking wet—dunked in the cooler. And just when you wanted a drink!

The End

SPR
RO
44

You take a deep breath and jump into the swirling waters. Immediately you're carried under. A second later your shoulder slams against a submerged boulder. For a moment you twirl like a top, unable to tell up from down. Your life jacket brings you to the surface, and you get a gasp of air before the seething waters pull you down once more.

Again you surface, surrounded by foam and spray. You can't see where the current is taking you. Your strength is waning. Like a half-dead animal, you float, weakly paddling. Then, though you're hardly able to think, you become aware that the waters have calmed.

Turn to page 115.

"I think it's too risky—we'd better do what the sign says and carry our canoe," you say.

"Definitely," Jenny says.

Bass reluctantly agrees, and the three of you beach the canoe and start carrying it up the steep winding path along the side of the canyon. It's hard work, but eventually you reach the high point in the trail. You set the canoe down and plant yourselves on a broad ledge overlooking the river.

There you sit, eating sandwiches, staring at the violent waters below.

"You wanted us to paddle through that stuff?" Jenny says to Bass.

"I didn't know it would be that rough," he answers.

"It's pretty to look at," you say. "The way the water flies up when it hits the rocks."

"Can you imagine what that would do to a canoe?" Bass says.

"And to us," Jenny adds.

"We'd be a little late getting back to camp," you say.

Turn to page 41.

SPRING ROCK
44
6:11
6
00

Once again you take the ball up the court. While you try to set the offense, it's stripped from behind by the player guarding you. He drives down and whips it over to their six-foot-nine center, who leaps up and jams the ball home. Windham 6, Spring Rock 0. This is not what you had in mind.

Groans rise from the Spring Rock fans. Two Windham students hold up a big sign: SPRING ROCK: GO BACK TO YOUR PLAYPEN.

On the next drive a Spring Rock player shoots a three-pointer and misses. Again Windham moves the ball down the court. But they misfire, and the ball sails out-of-bounds.

Spring Rock has the ball. Over to you. You drive down, pass it to your forward, get free from your man. Your forward gives it back to you, you move in for the layup and get hacked. Two free throws for you.

All eyes on you.

You sink one. Then you miss one. Windham 6, Spring Rock 1. At least you're on the board.

Turn to page 110.

Your second and last year at Spring Rock you find that you're working harder in your studies and harder on the court. You're playing point guard, hoping to beat your last season's average of scoring twelve points a game. And Coach Bartok says that Spring Rock has a chance at its first undefeated season in history.

School life is going pretty well. You're popular enough to have been defeated by only two votes in the election for class president. You have only one worry. College costs have gone up so much that, if you're not offered a scholarship, you won't be able to afford to go.

Mr. Dawkins, Spring Rock's principal, has an unusual custom. He calls in every student, one by one, for a personal conference during the fall term of each school year. You're not surprised, a few weeks after school starts, to be told to report to his office. After keeping you waiting in the hall a few minutes, he asks you in and tells you to have a seat.

Mr. Dawkins is a small, thin-faced man who always wears oversize tortoiseshell eyeglasses that make his eyes look too big. He looks like a nerd, but the word is that he's a no-nonsense kind of guy. As he sits across the desk from you and picks up your folder, you feel the same way you do when you go to the dentist. Maybe worse. Your marks haven't been as high as you'd hoped. He'll probably say that just being a good basketball player isn't enough to get you a college scholarship.

Turn to page 80.

In the fall, when Windham's next basketball season gets underway, you start playing better from your first day on the court. By the end of the season the coach is putting you in every game. But it's not until your last year at Windham that you really begin to shine.

You're bigger and stronger now. You've got more confidence. You're more focused on the game. And you keep on improving right through the season. The whole team improves too. Everyone works closely together when you're out on the court. When you look for the ball, it's there. When you need to unload it, there's somebody free to help you out. That's why Windham goes undefeated against a lineup of some of the best teams in the state. And why they're now facing the biggest challenge of all: today's game with Lakeville will decide the state championship.

There's a lot of hype leading up to the game. The truth is that you feel a little nervous. And when you hear there are going to be college scouts in attendance, you feel a knot in the pit of your stomach.

Go on to the next page.

You feel better once you're out on the court warming up with the guys. Although Lakeville has been a powerhouse the last few years, Windham is almost even odds to win. Your coach says you've got the momentum to carry you through. You concentrate on that as you go out on the court.

Suddenly the moment you've been dreaming of arrives: tip-off! An official lofts the ball into the air, and the big game has begun.

Go on to the next page.

Your center leaps and bats it to your shooting guard who starts to dribble downcourt. You run ahead and set up a defender, then cut to the left, take a pass, and drain it for the first two points of the game. Windham 2, Lakeside 0. The action continues at breakneck pace, and the lead seesaws back and forth throughout the rest of the first half.

Turn to page 4.

"Let's try to sneak in," you say.

The others agree to go for it, and the three of you back off and then bike down the road until you're around a curve, out of sight of the guardhouse. You ditch your bikes behind some thick bushes, then cut through the woods. Soon you arrive at the iron grill fence that runs around the Gordon property.

You walk along the fence. After about fifty yards you reach a place where you can catch glimpses of the house through the trees. The house is a nice white colonial—big, but not as big as you'd imagined it might be. A three-car garage and a little guest house lie beyond it. The main house has a porch that looks over a big lawn and fine old trees.

"This is as good a place to climb over as any," says Bob, looking up at the top of the fence.

"Those spikes are no problem," says Fred. "Just step in the space between them, use them to lever yourself over, then jump. Someone give me a boost."

"Okay, but how will the last one get over?" Bob asks.

"Easy," you say. "I'll go last. When you two are inside, cup your hands through the bars and make steps for me."

In a minute the three of you are over the fence and on the ground.

"Now what?" Bob says.

Turn to page 39.

Windham has the ball, passing around the perimeter. Their center shoots from outside. A Spring Rock player blocks it but is called for goaltending. Windham sinks both of their free throws. Windham 8, Spring Rock 1.

You see a discouraged look on a teammate's face. "Go, go, go," you yell, and pass him the ball.

Down the court. You set a pick. A short pass. Your teammate hooks it in. "That's the way."

Get back down to defend. Step up the pace, turn things around.

A teammate snares a crosscourt pass. He rifles it out to you, but high. You leap up and amazingly pull it down with one hand. You have a terrific urge to slam-dunk for your first time in a game.

If you try to slam-dunk,
turn to page 8.

If you decide to play it safe and go in
for a layup, turn to page 44.

A couple of weeks later you arrive at the Art Stegler Basketball Camp, located in the mountains of northern Arizona. Stegler was a former NBA star, and his camp draws young players from all over the country.

There are six courts, two coaches, and six junior coaches, most of them on summer vacation from the schools and colleges where they coach during the winter. The weather is gre t, the scenery is pretty, and there are quite a few kids you can imagine making friends with.

Despite all this, the camp doesn't impress you. There are several bunkhouses, with too many narrow bunks squeezed into each one. Training seems pretty casual. Most of the coaches don't seem to care whether you work hard or not. As for Art Stegler himself, you learn that he hardly ever shows up. To make matters worse, the food tastes like cardboard or dog food depending on what day of the week it is. Well, maybe not that bad.

Camp lasts six weeks. The only break is a one-day wilderness trip your second Sunday there.

On the day of the trip, a bus takes you and a group of other campers and one of the coaches to the High Point Lodge on the Tapis River. There are a number of trails and campsites nearby. Most of the campers want to go hiking, but you and a couple of kids you've made friends with—Jenny Cracas and Bass Walker—decide to take a canoe down the river.

Turn to page 66.

You swallow your pride and just shrug at Clive's taunting. "Got to go, Clive," you say, and head for the door without buying anything.

The next morning you, Fred, and Bob bike out to Sequoia Road. A different guard is on duty, but you give him your names and he waves you in.

A few minutes later you're doing something you'd never dreamed of: playing basketball with Jeffrey Gordon!

It's the three of you against Jeffrey. But none of you can even get a shot off against him, much less a field goal. At least until he lets up. Then it's really fun, and every once in a while he'll take the ball and stop the play while he points out something—like calling your attention to a gesture or a glance that is telegraphing your moves or shots, explaining how you shouldn't always start dribbling the moment you get the ball, or showing you how to pivot before moving off.

Turn to page 55.

GORDAN
33
5

Someone is calling your name. It's Bass, standing waist-deep in water a few yards away, motioning to you! You swim a few strokes toward him. He wades closer to meet you, grabs your hand, and pulls you into shallower water. Groggy, aching, you manage to stand. The two of you wade to shore, a grassy bank safe from harm. Jenny is lying there, propped up against a dead log, one of her arms bent in an unnatural way. She manages a smile.

You and Bass heave yourself onto the shore beside her. The canoe has completely disappeared, and none of you is in shape to walk far, much less swim. There's nothing to do but wait for help, but at least you're safe. And Jenny, grinning through her pain, makes you and Bass smile.

"Well" she says, "we got dunked, and we got slammed. I guess you could say we got slam-dunked."

The End

"Through? Nonsense." Mr. Dawkins practically jumps out of his chair. He peers at you over his glasses. "You're young. You're intelligent. You can work. You can save money. You can do something special. You can do things next year that will change you from a long shot to a sure shot."

He walks around the desk and shakes your hand. "You're a kid who's going places, and don't you forget it. All you have to do is keep moving."

The End

A week later, you get a phone call at school—an offer for a basketball scholarship at the state university. You're so amazed and delighted that when you get home you practice three-pointers until after dark.

The End

ABOUT THE AUTHOR

EDWARD PACKARD is a graduate of Princeton University and Columbia Law School. He developed the unique storytelling approach used in the Choose Your Own Adventure series while thinking up stories for his children Caroline, Andrea, and Wells.

ABOUT THE ILLUSTRATOR

TOM LA PADULA graduated from Parsons School of Design with a BFA and earned his MFA from Syracuse University.

For over a decade Tom has illustrated for national and international magazines, advertising agencies, and publishing houses. Besides his illustrating, Tom is on the faculty of Pratt Institute, where he teaches a class in illustration.

During the spring of 1992, his work was exhibited in the group show "The Art of the Baseball Card" at the Baseball Hall of Fame in Cooperstown, New York. In addition, the corporation Johnson & Johnson recently acquired one of Tom's illustrations for their private collection.

Mr. La Padula has illustrated *The Luckiest Day of Your Life, Secret of the Dolphins, Scene of the Crime, The Secret of Mystery Hill, Soccer Star,* and *Gunfire at Gettysburg* in the Choose Your Own Adventure series. He resides in New Rochelle, New York, with his wife, son, and daughter.

Packard, Edward

Sky-jam!

DUE DATE	BRODART	05/95	3.50
MAR 13 '96			
NOV 6 '96			
FEB 19 '97			
OCT 01 '97			
DEC 01 '97			